Dear Parents:

Ready Reader Storybooks™ have been developed with your kinder-
garten through second-grader in mind. This series is designed to
encourage young readers to begin to read alone, thus increasing basic
reading skills. The simple stories have easy-to-follow plots, and the
bright, colorful illustrations add to the fun, and provide the visual
appeal that helps to promote and enhance your youngster's reading
experience.

The stories in this series vary in subject matter and style, so your
child will be sure to find stories of interest. The large type is easy to
read, and the format is just the right size for small hands to hold.
The Ready Reader Storybooks™ will delight while developing and
encouraging your child's independent reading skills.

Rosie's Two Left Feet

Written by Jean Davis Callaghan
Illustrated by Florie Freshman

Modern Publishing
A Division of Unisystems, Inc.
New York, New York 10022

It is Grandpa's birthday.
Rosie and her family are going to
his party.

"Here are your new party shoes," Mother says.

Rosie is happy about going to a grown-up party, and about having new party shoes.

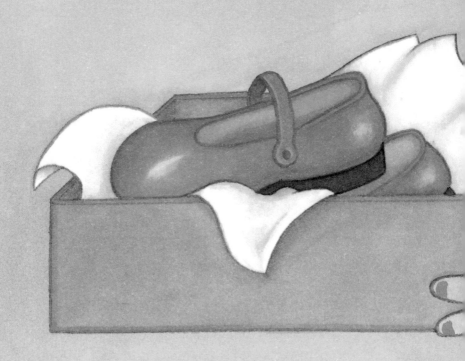

Rosie and her sister, Anne, finish getting ready.

"My new shoes feel funny," Rosie says.

"Oh, dear," says Mother. "The store gave us two left foot shoes. We will have to return them in the morning."

Perhaps school shoes will look nice with Rosie's party dress.

No, they don't. How about sneakers?

Where are they?

"There they are!" says Rosie.
"Oh, Pups, you silly dog!"

"Those sneakers don't look very nice with your party dress, either," says Mother.

Anne has an idea!

She shines her old party shoes
that she has outgrown.

Anne saves the day!

Her old shoes look brand-new
again. So clean. Such shiny
buckles.

"Thank you, Anne," says Rosie.
Rosie is so proud.
Anne even finds a ribbon to
match the shoes.

Now everyone can go to the party.

Happy birthday, Grandpa!